対訳

POEMS OF EXORCISM

厄除け詩集

井伏鱒二
Masuji Ibuse

ウィリアム・Ｉ・エリオット
西原克政
訳

Translated by
William I. Elliott
Katsumasa Nishihara

田畑書店
*Tabata Shoten, Tokyo*

# 目　次

訳詩　*TRANSLATIONS*

# 厄除け詩集

*POEMS OF EXORCISM*

# な　だ　れ

峯の雪が裂け
雪がなだれる
そのなだれに
熊が乗つてゐる
あぐらをかき
安閑と
莨をすふやうな恰好で
そこに一ぴき熊がゐる

# AVALANCHE

Snow on the summit cracks
and slides down in an avalanche.
A bear rides
the avalanche.
It sits cross-legged
making itself at home,
as if smoking a pipe.
There's a bear there, that's for sure.

## つくだ煮の小魚

ある日　雨の晴れまに
竹の皮に包んだつくだ煮が
水たまりにこぼれ落ちた
つくだ煮の小魚達は
その一ぴき一ぴきを見てみれば
目を大きく見開いて
環になつて互にからみあつてゐる
鰭も尻尾も折れてゐない
顎の呼吸するところには　色つやさへある
そして　水たまりの底に放たれたが
あめ色の小魚達は
互に生きて返らなんだ

# SMALL FISH BOILED IN SOY SAUCE

One day with a break in the rain
some small fish soaked in soy
and wrapped in a bamboo sheath
fell into a puddle.
One by one they
opened their eyes wide
and got tangled up like garlands.
Their fins and tails were intact.
The gills where they breathed retained a fine luster.
Soon they sank to the bottom of the puddle
but these amber small fish
didn't come back alive.

## 歳末閑居

ながい梯子を廂にかけ
拙者はのろのろと屋根にのぼる
冷たいが棟瓦にまたがると
こりや甚だ眺めがよい

ところで今日は暮の三十日
ままよ大胆いつぷくしてゐると
平野屋は霜どけの路を来て
今日も留守だねと帰つて行く

拙者はのろのろと屋根から降り
梯子を部屋の窓にのせる
これぞシーソーみたいな設備かな
子供を相手に拙者シーソーをする

どこに行つて来たと拙者は子供にきく

# A QUIET LIFE AT THE END OF THE YEAR

Setting a long ladder against the eaves,
I climb onto the roof slowly.
It is cold but if I sit astraddle the tile's crest
I can command a fine view.

Today is, by the way, December 30th.
Oh, well, while I'm taking a break,
a master in Hiranoya comes boldly along a slushy road
and goes away saying, "No one's home today, either."

I slowly climb down from the roof
and put the ladder against the window of the room,
wondering if it would be like a seesaw
to see a scene where I play with my child.

I ask my son where he has been.

母ちやんとそこを歩いて来たといふ
凍<sup>こご</sup>えるやうに寒かつたかときけば
凍えるやうに寒かつたといふ

母ちやんとそこを歩いて来たといふ
凍（こご）えるやうに寒かつたかときけば
凍えるやうに寒かつたといふ

Then he says he has just come back from taking a walk
  with his mother.
And I ask if it was freezingly cold.
He says, "Yeah, it was freezingly cold."

.

# 石　地　蔵


風は冷たくて
もうせんから降りだした
大つぶな霰（あられ）は　ぱらぱらと
三角畑のだいこんの葉に降りそそぎ
そこの畦みちに立つ石地蔵は
悲しげに目をとぢ掌（て）をひろげ
家を追ひ出された子供みたいだ
（よほど寒さうぢやないか）


お前は幾つぶもの霰を掌に受け
お前の耳たぶは凍傷（しもやけ）だらけだ
霰は　ぱらぱらと
お前のおでこや肩に散り
お前の一張羅（いつちやうら）のよだれかけは
もうすつかり濡れてるよ

# A STONE STATUE OF JIZO

The wind is chilly and cold.
It began raining quite some time ago.
Large snow pellets have started sprinkling down
on the daikon leaves in a triangular field.
Beside a raised footpath there is a stone statue of Jizo
with its sad eyes closed and open hands,
looking like a child kicked out of a house.
(It seemed terribly cold.)

A lot of snow pellets are falling on your palms.
You've got a lot of chilblains on your earlobes.
Snow pellets are sprinkling
your forehead and shoulders.
Your smart bib, your only clothing,
is already soaked.

# 逸　　題


今宵は仲秋明月
初恋を偲ぶ夜
われら万障くりあはせ
よしの屋で独り酒をのむ


春さん蛸のぶつ切りをくれえ
それも塩でくれえ
酒はあついのがよい
それから枝豆を一皿


ああ　蛸のぶつ切りは臍みたいだ
われら先づ腰かけに坐りなほし
静かに酒をつぐ
枝豆から湯気が立つ


今宵は仲秋明月

# A LOST TITLE

Tonight a harvest moon —
and a time for missing our first love.
But forgetting everything,
we drink alone tonight in Yoshinoya.

*Say, Haru, how about some chopped octopus?*
*With salt, please.*
*And make sure the sake's hot.*
*And a dish of green soybeans.*

*Ha! The octopi look like belly buttons.*
So, we sit down and sit tall
and quietly pour the sake.
The soybeans breathe steam.

Tonight a harvest moon —

初恋を偲ぶ夜
われら万障くりあはせ
よしの屋で独り酒をのむ

（新橋よしの屋にて）

and a time for missing our first love.
But forgetting everything,
we drink alone tonight in Yoshinoya.

(At Yoshinoya, Shimbashi)

# 冬 の 池 畔

―――甲州大正池―――


大正池に来れば
池の堤のさむさかな


今年は鴨がたくさんゐる
堤に雉が一羽ゐる
私は釣竿をとり出して
水ぎはに降りて寒鮒を釣る


このどぶ釣の釣竿は
人から借りてきた古手かな


私は慢性の腸カタル
手袋をはめてマスクをかけ
懐炉の灰を入れなほした

# ONE WINTER DAY BY A POND

— At Taisho Pond in the Koshu district —

When I get to Taisho Pond
it's severely cold on the bank.

Plenty of wild ducks have come this year.
There is a single pheasant on the bank.
Taking out a pole, I go down to the edge
and fish up a wintry crucian carp.

This fishing pole good for 'ditch mud'
is a used article borrowed from my friend.

As a matter of fact I have an old problem called intestinal
  catarrh,
so I'm wearing gloves and a mask
and carrying a pocket warmer filled with warm ashes.

堤に雉が三羽舞ひ下りた
私は虫くひの釣竿を持ち
案山子のやうに立つてゐる

Three pheasants have alighted on the bank.

I just stand alone like a scarecrow

holding my fishing pole riddled with worm holes.

## 按摩をとる

ここは甲州下部鉱泉の源泉館
その二階の一室である
御一泊は　一等四円五十銭
二等三円五十銭
三等二円五十銭と書いてある
私は右枕に寝ころんで
按摩（あんま）に肩を揉ましてゐる
按摩は毛糸の袖なしを着て
ロイド眼鏡をかけてゐる
彼の目にはまつ毛も目蓋（まぶた）もない
その目はまるでコスモスの実の一粒である
私が「青い鳥」を朗読してゐると
しかしそのコスモスの実から
じつとりと涙が出る

（下部町源泉館にて）

# RECEIVING A MASSAGE

I'm staying in a second floor room
of the Gensen Inn in the Koshu Shimobe Spas.
Some notes say a first-grade room is 4 yen 50 sen,
a second-grade 3 yen 50 sen
and a third-grade 2 yen 50 sen per night.
Lying on a futon on my right-side, my head on a pillow,
I have a masseur massage my shoulder.
He wears a woolen vest
and Lloyd glasses.
His eyes have no lashes or eyelids
and are like the nuts of the cosmos.
While I'm reading *The Bluebird* aloud,
tears spill dripping
out of the nuts of the cosmos.

(At the Gensen Inn in the town of Shimobe)

## 寒夜母を思ふ

今日ふるさとの母者から
ちよつといいものを送つて来た
百両のカハセを送つて来た
ひといきつけるといふものだらう

ところが母者は手紙で申さるる
お前このごろ横着(わうちやく)に候
これをしみじみ御覧ありたしと
私の六つのときの写真を送つて来た

私は四十すぎたおやぢである
古ぼけた写真に用はない
私は夜ふけて原稿書くのが商売だ
写真などよりドテラがいい

私は着たきりの着たきり雀

# THINKING OF MY MOTHER ON A COLD NIGHT

My mother sent me something nice
from my hometown today.
It was a money order worth a million yen.
Great! Now I'm on Easy Street.

But my mother says in her letter:
I've recently become a goldbrick;
I ought to take a good look at this, she says
of the photo of me at age six she has sent.

I'm now over forty, a man past middle age,
and I don't want a time-worn photograph anymore.
My business is writing a manuscript late at night,
so I would like a padded kimono rather than a photo.

The only clothes I have to wear are the ones on my back.

襟垢は首にひんやりとする
それで机の前に坐るにも
かうして前こごみに坐ります

今宵は零下何度の寒さだらう
ペンのインクも凍てついた
鼻水ばかり流れ出る
それでも詩を書く痩せ我慢

母者は手紙で申さるる
お前の痩せ我慢は無駄ごとだ
小説など何の益にか相成るや
田舎に帰れよと申さるる

母者は性来ぐちつぽい
私を横着者だと申さるる
私に山をば愛せと申さるる
土地をば愛せと申さるる
祖先を崇めよと申さるる

Dirt on the collar feels cool on my neck.
That's why I tend to bend forward this way
when I sit at my desk.

How many degrees below zero is it tonight?
The ink in my pen is already frozen.
My nose keeps running.
I try to write a poem anyway, never saying die.

My mother says in her letter:
My false courage is useless; It can't be said
a novel makes a real contribution to the world;
you'd better come back home as soon as possible.

My mother is by birth a peevish person.
She says I'm a shirker;
I should love mountains;
I should love the land
and that I should honor my ancestors.

母者は性来のしわんばう
私に積立貯金せよと申さるる
お祖師様を拝めと申さるる
悲しいかなや母者びと

My mother is a born penny pincher.

She says I should save by installments

and that I should worship the Venerable Nichiren.

Oh, what a pitiable fate to be born a mother!

## かなめの生垣

かなめの生垣に寄れば
目に疑ふ　白き木瓜[ぼけ]の花
私はマントの襟を立て
地に沿うてとぶみそさざいを見る

# A HEDGE AS A CORNERSTONE

Coming close to a hedge as a cornerstone,

I can't believe my eyes, seeing the flowers of a Japanese
   quince.

I just turn up the collar of my cloak

and see a wren just above the ground.

## つばなつむうた
### （わらべうた）


往（い）んでやろ往んでやろ
空籠さげて往んでやろ
ハツタビラへ来てみたが
カケスが鳴いて坊主原（ぼうずつばら）
草刈り草刈り来てみたが
刈りとるこぐち籠目をもれた
空籠さげて往んでやろ
──これで十五本目ぢや

# A SONG OF PICKING THE EARS OF REEDS

(Nursery Rhyme)

I'll come home, come home,
with my empty basket, I'll come home.
I'm now in Hatsutabira but I've found myself
on a bare field with only a jay cawing.
I'm just here to mow with a sickle
but a harvest of reeds slip through the basket.
Then I'll come home with my empty basket —
gosh, this will be the fifteenth time.

# 顎

けふ顎のはづれた人を見た
電車に乗つてゐると
途端にその人の顎がはづれた
その人は狼狽へたが
もう間にあはなかつた
ぱつくり口があいたきりで
舌を出し涙をながした
気の毒やら可笑しいやら
私は笑ひ出しさうになつた

「ほろをん　ほろをん」
橋の下の菖蒲は誰が植ゑた菖蒲ぞ
ほろをん　ほろをん

私は電車を降りてからも
込みあげて来る笑ひを殺さうとした

# JAW

I've seen a man's jaw out of joint today.
Just as I sat in the train,
his jaw in front of me immediately went out of joint.
He panicked of course
but it was too late.
With his mouth agape,
he stuck out his tongue and cried.
Feeling pitiful and funny,
I nearly burst out laughing.

"Dangle-dangle."
Who planted sweet flags under the bridge?
Dangle-dangle.

Even after I got off the train,
I couldn't keep from laughing out loud.

## 山の図に寄せる


これは背戸（せど）の山の眺めである
鬼のとうすといふ名前の
大岩の上から見た景色
わが故郷の山々である


右に見えるは中条の山
明日（あす）は雨ぢやといふ夜さは
山のきれめで稲光りする
左に見えるは広瀬の山
近くに見えるは大林寺山


もう一つのこの画面
左に見えるは四川（しがは）の山
夏日夕立が来るときは
先づこの山の背に雲が寄る
右に見えるは芋原（いもばら）の山

# TO DRAWINGS OF MOUNTAINS

This is a view of the mountains in Sedo:
a landscape seen from the top of a big rock
called 'Ogre's Dagger';
those are the mountains in my hometown;

To the right can be seen the mountains in Chujo;
at night when there'll be rain tomorrow
lightning flashes around the saddle of the mountains;
to the left can be seen the mountain in Hirose;
closer yet is Mt. Dairinji.

There's another drawing:
to the left can be seen the mountains in Shigawa;
when a shower comes down on a summer's day,
clouds will gather around this ridge first;
to the right can be seen the mountains in Imobara;

手前に見えるは七曲り

何でもないやうなこの山々
望郷の念とやら起させる
こんな筈はないと思ふのに
どうにもならないことである

even nearer is a winding road.

These mountains, though looking like nothing,
arouse homesickness.
I really can't believe this
but nothing can be done about it.

# 訳　　詩
*TRANSLATIONS*

## 題袁氏別業

賀　知　章

主 人 不 相 識
偶 坐 為 林 泉
莫 謾 愁 沽 酒
囊 中 自 有 錢

主人ノ名前ハ知ラナイガ
庭ガミタサニチヨトコシカケタ
サケヲ買フトテオ世話ハムヨウ
ワシガサイフニゼニガアル

# ON MR. YUAN'S OTHER BUSINESS

*Ho Chih-chang*

I don't know the name of the master of this house
but I just want to sit down and look at the garden.
Don't worry and I'll buy some sake
because there's some money in my wallet.

## 照鏡見白髪

張 九齢

宿 昔 青 雲 志
蹉 跎 白 髪 年
誰 知 明 鏡 裏
形 影 自 相 憐

シユツセシヨウト思ウテキタニ
ドウカウスル間ニトシバカリヨル
ヒトリカガミニウチヨリミレバ
皺ノヨツタヲアハレムバカリ

# LOOKING AT MY GRAY HAIR IN A MIRROR

*Chang Chiu-ling*

Though I've tried to succeed in life,
all I can manage is ageing year after year.
I look into a mirror as if attracted by it
and take pity on my wrinkle-lined face.

### 送朱大入秦

孟 浩 然

遊 人 五 陵 去
宝 剣 直 千 金
分 手 脱 相 贈
平 生 一 片 心

コンドキサマハオ江戸ヘユキヤル
オレガカタナハ千両道具
コレヲシンゼルセンベツニ
ツネノ気性ハコレヂヤトオモヘ

# SEEING MY FRIEND OFF TO QIN

*Meng Hao-jan*

So you're going up to Edo.

My sword is a great thing easily worth a thousand in gold

but I'll give it to you as a parting gift.

So take as good a care of yourself as of this sword.

# 春　　暁

孟　浩　然

春 眠 不 覚 暁
処 処 聞 啼 鳥
夜 来 風 雨 声
花 落 知 多 少

ハルノネザメノウツツデ聞ケバ
トリノナクネデ目ガサメマシタ
ヨルノアラシニ雨マジリ
散ツタ木ノ花イカホドバカリ

# SPRING DAWN

*Meng Hao-jan*

I waken with bird song,
still half-asleep, in spring dawn.
Rain mingles with the stormy night.
I wonder how many blossoms have fallen
   from the tree.

洛陽道献呂四郎中

儲　光　羲

大　道　直　如　髪
春　日　佳　気　多
五　陵　貴　公　子
双　双　鳴　玉　珂

ミチハマツスグ先ヅ髪スヂダ
ドウトモ云ハレヌコノ春ゲシキ
ヤシキヤシキノ若トノ衆ガ
サソフクツワノオトリンリント

# TO THE TUNE OF A FLUTE FOR A YOUNG PRINCE

*Chu Guang-xi*

This avenue in the capital is straight like hair.
The air is bustling with merriment on a spring day.
Princes ride their horses out of their mansions,
their small bells on the fringes jingling charmingly.

# 長　安　道

儲　光　羲

鳴　鞭　過　酒　肆
袨　服　遊　倡　門
百　万　一　時　尽
含　情　無　片　言

馬ニムチウチサカヤヲスギテ
綾ヤ錦デヂヨロヤニアソブ
タツタイチヤニセンリヤウステテ
カネヲツカツタ顔モセヌ

# ON THE ROAD TO CHANGAN

*Chu Guang-xi*

Whipping my horse past a tavern,

I visit a brothel gorgeously decked out.

Wasting a thousand pieces of gold in one night,

I pretend not to be spending any money at all.

# 復　　愁

杜　　甫

万国尚戎馬
故園今奈何
昔帰相識少
蚤已戦場多

ドコモカシコモイクサノサカリ
オレガ在所ハイマドウヂヤヤラ
ムカシ帰ツタトキニサヘ
ズキブン馴染ガウタレタサウナ

# RESURGENT MELANCHOLY

*Tu Fu*

The war's raging everywhere.

I wonder if my hometown is all right now.

Even a long time ago when I was home,

I heard that my old buddies had been killed in battle.

# 逢　俠　者

銭　　起

燕趙悲歌士
相逢劇孟家
寸心言不尽
前路日将斜

イヅレナダイノ顔ヤクタチガ
トモニカタラフ文七ガイヘ
ダテナハナシノマダ最中ニ
マヘノチマタハ日ガクレル

# MEETING A CERTAIN KNIGHT OF
## THE TOWN
### *Ch'ien Ch'i*

Bosses from several districts

gather at the gambler Bunhichi's.

Even as they go on talking stuff and nonsense

night has already fallen on the street in front of his house.

## 答 李 澣

韋 応 物

林 中 観 易 罷
渓 上 対 鷗 間
楚 俗 饒 詞 客
何 人 最 往 還

ヤマニカクレテ易ミルヒトハ
タニノカモメト静カニクラス
ココノ国ニハ詩人ガ多イ
タレガトリワケ来テアソブ

# A LETTER IN REPLY TO MY FRIEND

*Wei Yingwu*

A fortune-teller like a hermit in the mountain
lives quietly in the valley with a gull.
There are a lot of poets in this part of the country.
I wonder just who will come and pay him a visit.

# 聞　雁

韋応物

故園眇何処
帰思方悠哉
准南秋雨夜
高斎聞雁来

ワシガ故郷ハハルカニ遠イ
帰リタイノハカギリモナイゾ
アキノ夜スガラサビシイアメニ
ヤクシヨデ雁ノ声ヲキク

# THE CRY OF A WILD GOOSE

*Wei Yingwu*

My hometown is too far away.

I wish I could go back right now.

All night long autumn rain has been falling.

From the town hall I hear a wild goose honking.

# 静 夜 思

李　白

牀 前 看 月 光
疑 是 地 上 霜
拳 頭 望 山 月
低 頭 思 故 郷

ネマノウチカラフト気ガツケバ
霜カトオモフイイ月アカリ
ノキバノ月ヲミルニツケ
ザイシヨノコトガ気ニカカル

# NIGHT THOUGHTS IN QUIETUDE

*Li Po*

Finding myself in bed under a thick quilt,
I catch sight of moonlight that I could mistake for frost.
The moment I see the moon by the eaves
my hometown weighs so heavily on my mind.

## 田家春望

高　適

出 門 何 所 見
春 色 満 平 蕪
可 歎 無 知 己
高 陽 一 酒 徒

ウチヲデテミリヤアテドモナイガ
正月キブンガドコニモミエタ
トコロガ会ヒタイヒトモナク
アサガヤアタリデ大ザケノンダ

# A SPRING LANDSCAPE OF WILD FIELDS

*Kao Shih*

Leave the house and you'll just be at a loss.
The cheerful air of the New Year pervades everywhere.
Yet there's no one I particularly would like to see,
so I barhop too much around the Asagaya district.

秋夜寄丘二十二員外

韋応物

懐君属秋夜
散歩咏涼天
山空松子落
幽人応未眠

ケンチコヒシヤヨサムノバンニ
アチラコチラデブンガクカタル
サビシイ庭ニマツカサオチテ
トテモオマヘハ寝ニクウゴザロ

# TO MY CLOSEST FRIEND ON AN AUTUMN NIGHT

*Wei Yingwu*

Such a cold night makes me miss Kenchi.

People here and there in a bar are talking about literature.

A pinecone falls on a lonely garden,

so you find it hard to fall asleep.

## 別廬秦卿

司空曙

知有前期在
難分此夜中
無将故人酒
不及石尤風


ソレハサウダトオモウテヰルガ
コンナニ夜フケテカヘルノカ
サケノテマヘモアルダロガ
カゼガアレタトオモヘバスムゾ

# A FAREWELL TO CHING LU

*Ssu Kung Shu*

I understand what you insist on
but you're leaving so late at night.
Though you feel inept about my skill at preparing sake
you can manage it quite well just imagining it's a
　　stormy night.

# 勧　　酒

于 武 陵

勧 君 金 屈 巵
満 酌 不 須 辞
花 発 多 風 雨
人 生 足 別 離

コノサカヅキヲ受ケテクレ
ドウゾナミナミツガシテオクレ
ハナニアラシノタトヘモアルゾ
「サヨナラ」ダケガ人生ダ

# A DRINKING SONG

*Yu Wu-ling*

Please take this cup
and let me fill it with wine.
Wind scatters the petals.
Life is nothing but saying good-bye.

## 古 別 離

孟　郊


欲　別　牽　郎　衣
郎　今　到　何　処
不　恨　帰　来　遅
莫　向　臨　邛　去


ワカレニクサニソデヒキトメテ
オマヘコレカライヅクヘユキヤル
カヘリノオソイヲ恨ミハセヌガ
ヨシハラヘンガ気ニカカル

# EVENTUAL SEPARATION

*Meng Jiao*

Pulling at your sleeve because the parting is wrenching,

I wonder where you'll be going from now on.

I don't begrudge your coming back late

but I do mind about that Yoshiwara quarter.

## 登柳州蛾山

荒 山 秋 日 午
独 上 意 悠 悠
如 何 望 郷 処
西 北 是 融 州

アキノオンタケココノツドキニ
ヒトリノボレバハテナキオモヒ
ワシノ在所ハドコダカミエヌ
イヌキノカタハヒダノヤマ

# CLIMBING A CRAGGY MOUNTAIN IN LIUZHOU

*Liao Tsung-yuan*

Climbing up Mt. Ontake alone at nine in autumn,

I'm seized by boundless thoughts.

My hometown is nowhere to be seen from here.

In the northwest the Hida mountains are visible.

# 雨 滴 調

*AFTER THE MANNER OF A TUNE*
*OF DRIPPING RAINWATER*

# 渓　　流

今日はさつぱり釣れない
をとりの鮎も
一ぴき曳きころし
一ぴきは逃がした

でも釣りたい
糸のさきに
石ころをむすびつけ
かうして釣る真似をする

ごつごつ　ごろごろ
まさに手応へがある
カハセミのやつ
羨ましさうに見てゐるぞ

# MOUNTAIN STREAM

I've not caught any fish today.
As for *ayu* fish as live bait
I ended up letting one die from dragging it too hard
and losing another one.

But I still wanna go on fishing.
Tying a stone around the end of a line,
I imitate
dropping a line.

*Tap, tap. Roll, roll.*
I feel a sharp tug on the line for sure.
I can see a kingfisher
eyeing me enviously.

# 魚　　拓

（農家素描）


明日は五郎作宅では息子の法事
長男戦死　次男戦死　三男戦死
これをまとめて供養する

仏壇にそなへたお飾りは
どんぶりに盛りあげたこんにやくだま
その一つ一つがてらてらに光り
その色どりに添へたのは
霜に焦けた南天の葉

五郎作は太い足をなげ出して
踵の大あかぎれを治療中である
おかみさんが木綿針に木綿糸で
その大あかぎれを縫ひあはせてゐる

枕屏風には嘗て次男三男が競争の

# FISH PRINTS

### (A Sketch of a Farmhouse)

A memorial service for his deceased sons will be held tomorrow
at Gorosaku's. The eldest, second and third were all killed
in the war. One service will serve for the repose of all three.

The offering on an altar
is a bowl of konnyaku balls.
Each one of them is shining lustrously.
To their coloring is added
a stem of frostbitten nandina leaves.

Gorosaku casually sticks out his fat legs
and gets the big chapped sores on his heels treated.
His wife is stitching up the wounds
with cotton thread in the eye of a needle.

Two fish prints are pasted on a bedside screen:

魚拓が二枚貼りつけてある

Those are the remains of what the second and the third
sons caught in their rivalry.

# か　す　み


広い広い沙漠である──
その夢のなかで私は
一人の口髭の男に逢つた
何といふぶざまなことか
彼は素裸になり四つばひになり
のそりのそりと這つて行く


「おい、ものども」と彼は云ふ
「我輩のあとからついて来い」
このとき一陣の風がわき起り
狂ほしく砂ぼこりが舞ひあがる
私は目をこすり目をこすり
砂ぼこりを浴びてゐる彼を見る


彼は尻を立てて這つて行く
その行手は遠く無際限に通じ

# MIST

It's a wide, wide desert —
I come upon a man with a mustache
in a dream.
What an unsightly sight it is
for him getting stark-naked down on all fours
and to go crawling sluggishly along.

He says, "Hey, men!"
"Follow me."
Then a gust of wind comes up
and a cloud of dust is wildly blown up.
Repeatedly rubbing my eyes,
I look at him all covered with dust.

He crawls about with his rear up
and his path leads to infinity in the distance.

かすむ流砂の大海原
「ものども、我輩につづけ」
彼は打ち振る尻尾もないままに
かすみのなかに消えて行く

It's a great wide ocean of quicksand in mist.

"Men, follow me!"

He, minus his own tail to wag,

disappears into the mist.

# つらら

場所は
甚九郎方裏手の水車小屋

毎年冬になると
その水車の輻につららが張る
敷布をちやうど干したやうに
輻のひろいひろいつららが張る

そのつららを表から見ろ
それからまた裏から見ろ
千羽がらすが写り出る
おのれの顔が写り出る

そこで息を吹きかけ耳を寄せろ
また息を吹きかけ耳を寄せろ
それを年の数だけくり返せ

# ICICLES

The place is a water mill
at the back of Jinkuro's house.

Every year in winter
icicles form on the spokes of the mill.
They look like sheets hung out for drying.
They're spreading really widely.

Look at them from the front
and look at them from the back.
A rook will be mirrored.
My face will be mirrored.

Now breathe out and keep your ear to them.
Breathe out again and keep your ear to them.
Do that again as many as your age.

それからつららを打ち砕け
この瞬間
骸骨が通り去る

場所は
甚九郎方裏手の水車小屋

Then break them to pieces.
At this moment
a skeleton passes by me.

The place is a water mill
at the back of Jinkuro's house.

# 勉三さん


金剛地端の勉三さんが
薄刃の鎌で
えいつとばかりに鶏の首をきつた
何といふ不思議——首のない鶏は
断末魔の羽ばたきで舞ひあがり
納屋の廂の上にむくろを置いた


ずゐぶん昔の話である
わが少年時代の出来事である

## BENZO-SAN

Benzo-san on the outskirts of Kongoji
cut off a chicken's head with one mighty blow
of a thin bladed sickle.
What an incredible thing — the headless chicken
flew up with a flap of its wings in the throes of death
and lay itself down dead on the eaves of a barn!

It's a story of days long gone.
It was an incident in my boyhood.

## 川原の風景


去年の水害に　流されそこねた
川土手のひとかたまり
あたりは一めんの小石原
誰いひ出したともなく敗戦島と呼ぶ

けふはその島に山羊がゐる
一株の　ひよろひよろの梅の木に
なぜか山羊は癇性に頭をこすりつけ
梅の花を散らしてゐる

# RIVER BEACH SCENERY

In last year's flood damage there was something not washed
   away,
which is a long lump of earth on a riverbank.
There stretches a beach of pebbles as far as the eye can see.
I don't know why but they call it a defeated island.

Today a goat is standing on this island.
For some reason or other the goat rubs its head angrily
against a single spindly *ume* tree
and scatters its blossoms.

# 緑　　蔭


池の水ぎはの立札に
「この池に投石すべからず──当寺住職謹言」
と書いてある


ところが池に石を投げこむと
どぶんといふ音がする
もう一つ投げこむと
どぶんといふ音がする
何か蘊蓄ありげな音ではないか
もう一つ投げこむと
これまた奥妙なる音ではないか


もう一つ大きな石を投げこむと
がらりと庫裡の障子をあけ
「こら待て、くせもの」
老僧が帯をしめながら

# THE SHADE OF A TREE

By the edge of a pond there's a notice board saying,
"Don't throw stones in this pond —
a warning from the head priest of this temple".

Anyway I do throw a stone in the pond
and hear a splash.
I throw another
and hear another splash.
It sounds like a tremendous fund of knowledge, doesn't it?
I throw yet another in it.
It sounds like an enchanting melody, doesn't it?

When I throw another big stone in it
someone opens a shoji of his living quarters
and says in a loud voice, "Hey, cut it out, you rascal!"
An old monk quickly rushes out of his den

おつとり刀の恰好でとび出して来た

while tying his obi.

# 蛙

勘三さん　勘三さん
畦道で一ぷくする勘三さん
ついでに煙管(きせる)を掃除した
それから蛙をつかまへて
煙管のやにをば丸薬にひねり
蛙の口に押しこんだ

迷惑したのは蛙である
田圃の水にとびこんだが
目だまを白黒させた末に
おのれの胃の腑を吐きだして
その裏返しになつた胃袋を
田圃の水で洗ひだした

この洗濯がまた一苦労である
その手つきはあどけない

# FROG

Kanzo-san, Kanzo-san,
Kanzo-san who had a smoke on a raised footpath
between rice fields cleaned his pipe in passing.
Then he caught a frog, coated a medicinal pill
with nicotine from his pipe
and put it in the frog's mouth.

The frog was really put out.
It jumped into the paddy
but, rolling its eyes up and down,
it finally spit out its own stomach
and began to wash its inside-out stomach
with the water.

It was quite a job washing it.
The way it used its hands was naive.

先づ胃袋を両手に受け
揉むが如くに拝むが如く
おのれの胃の腑を洗ふのだ
洗ひ終ると呑みこむのだ

It first wrapped the stomach with its palms,

which looked like it was telling beads.

It washed its stomach in earnest

and after washing it swallowed it.

## 歌　碑

明るい月夜です
岡にのぼれば
万朶の桜です
その木かげの
真新しい歌碑の刻字
「満月は
くるる空より……」

次は読めぬ
花かげにかくれ
頬打つ花吹雪に……

# A MONUMENT INSCRIBED WITH A WAKA

It's a bright moonlit night.
You climb up a hill
through a mass of blossoming cherry branches.
In the shade of a tree among them stands
a new monument inscribed with a waka:
"Full moon
out of the darkened sky…."

The rest is undecipherable
because the shadow of the tree hides it;
and a storm of falling cherry blossoms hits my cheeks.

# 春　　宵

大雅堂の主人
佐藤俊雄が溝(どぶ)に落ちた
──僕がうしろを振向くと
忽焉(こつえん)として彼は消えてゐた──
やがて佐藤の呻き声がした
どろどろの汚水の溝であつた
彼は溝から這ひあがり
全くひどいですなあ
くさいなあと泣声を出した
それからしよんぼり立つてゐたが
ポケツトの溝泥を摑み出した
実にくさくて近寄れない
気の毒だとはいふものの
暫時は笑ひがとまらなかつた

# EVENING IN SPRING

A master in Taigado,
Toshio Sato fell into a gutter —
When I looked back at him
he vanished as if by magic —
soon Sato's painful groan was heard.
It was a thick, sticky, filthy ditch.
He crawled out of it,
saying it was horrible
and crying how terribly it stunk.
And after a while he stood alone crestfallen
and took two handfuls of mud out of his pockets.
I couldn't get near him because of his bad smell.
I felt sorry for him
but I couldn't help but laugh a little.

# 拾 遺 抄
*GLEANINGS*

# 黒 い 蝶

青山さんがロケイションに行つたとき
崖のはなの平たい大きな石をはねのけた
そこの穴ぼこにいつぱい黒い蝶がゐた
何千びきとも知れぬ黒い蝶である
それが蠢き　ぱつと飛びたち
あくまでも空たかく舞ひあがつて行つた

# BLACK BUTTERFLIES

When Aoyama went to a certain place,
he moved aside a big, flat rock at the edge of a cliff.
There were a lot of black butterflies under the rock:
Myriads of black butterflies you can have never imagined.
They swarmed, flew off
and exploded way up into the distant sky.

## 縄 な ひ 機

故郷の木下夕爾君の詩「東京行」を
読んで故郷の近江卓爾君に。

君が縄なひ機を買つたことは
をととしの君の手紙で知つた
君の操縦する縄なひ機は
夜汽車の走るやうな音を出し
君を旅に誘ひ出さうとする
そのことは去年の君の手紙で知つた

なぜ縄なひを始めたのだらう
僕は不思議なことに思つてゐた
けふ木下君のよこした詩を読んで
漸く君の意中を量り得た

君は東京見物に来たがつてゐる
旅費を稼がうとして縄をなふが

# A STRAW ROPE-TWISTING MACHINE

To Takuji Omi in my hometown after reading
Yuji Kinoshita's poem "A Trip to Tokyo"

I knew from your letter two years ago

that you'd bought a straw rope-making machine.

The machine you're supposed to operate

sounds like a night train running

and invites you out for a trip.

I knew that from your letter last year.


I thought it strange

that you'd begun to twist rope.

But having read Kinoshita's letter today

I can read your mind at long last.


You're willing to come and do the sights of Tokyo.

You twist a rope so as to earn traveling expenses,

旅費がたまりかけると汽車賃があがる
「縄なひ機械を踏む速度では
とても物価に追ひつけない……
なひあげた縄の長さは
北海道にも達するだらう……」
木下君はさういふ風に書いてゐる

僕は近く田舎に出かけるので
君の縄なひ機も見て来たい
汽車のやうな音がするのでは
紅殻塗りの旧式ではないだらうか
ともかく眼福の栄にあづかりたい

but even as you almost save up enough money train expenses
   are increasing.
"Even with the speed in which I step on the pedal of
this machine I can't catch up with commodity prices…
The length of a rope that I've twisted so far would reach
   Hokkaido…",
Kinoshita writes in the above.


I'm going back to my hometown soon,
so I'd like to see your straw rope-making machine.
If it sounds like a train, I wonder if
it's a reddish-brown painted, old-fashioned one.
I hope I'll have a wonderful surprise and a feast to the eyes.

## シンガポール所見

——戦争中、徴用されてシンガポールに住む。
某日、意外にもキリネー・ロードにて、東京
新宿中村屋のボースさんを見る。


走る走る——一人の印度人が

紫外線よけの眼鏡をかけ

いま熱狂の歓声をあげ

絵から抜け出た韋駄天だ

いっさんに自動車を追つて行く


その車蓋のない自動車に

これは意外

にこにこ笑ひながら

やはり紫外線よけの眼鏡をかけ

新宿中村屋のボースさんが乗つてゐる


自動車の行手には

印度人集会場の草原に　たくさんの人だかりだ

# MY IMPRESSIONS OF SINGAPORE

— I was in Singapore via the draft during the war.
One day on Killiney Road I unexpectedly saw Bose-san
who I'd seen in Nakamuraya, Shinjuku, Japan

Oh, running, running — an Indian,

wearing a pair of sunglasses,

now madly shouting with joy,

running at lightning speed as if out of a manga frame,

is chasing a car as fast as his legs can carry him.

In that roofless car —

Oh, my gosh! —

smiling a sweet smile,

wearing a pair of sunglasses just as sweetly,

is Bose-san in Nakamuraya, Shinjuku.

Ahead of the car

a crowd of Indians have gathered in a field.

見よ──青空を──あの集会堂の尖塔に
翩翻<ruby>翩翻<rt>へんぽん</rt></ruby>としてひるがへる印度独立の三色旗

Oh, look at that: the blue sky and in the steeple of an
   assembly hall
the tricolor flag of Indian independence is fluttering in
   the wind.

## 再疎開途上

　　　　鳥取駅のプラットホームに
　　　　妻子と共に一夜ごろ寝する。


おい　僕はいま何か云つたらう
「きやあッ」と云はなかつたかね
目がさめた途端
あのシグナルの青い灯を
焼夷弾のはぜる光と思つたのだ
僕は寒さで目がさめたのだ
蚤で目がさめたのかもわからない
おい　大変な蚤ではないか
プラットホームには
こんなに蚤が沢山ゐるものだらうか
あれを御覧　あの防空頭巾をかぶつた人も
寝ながら腕をかいてゐる
あそこの　鉄兜を枕元に置いてゐる人も
ぼりぼり首すぢをかいてゐる

# ON MY WAY TO EVACUATING TO MY HOMETOWN AGAIN IN WARTIME

I sleep on the bench with my wife and son
for one night on a platform in Tottori Station.


Hey, I wonder what I have said just now.

I haven't said "Yuk!", have I?

The moment I wake up,

I take the blue light of that signal

for the light of an incendiary bomb.

I think I wake up because of the cold.

I might have woken up because of fleas.

Oh, boy! A lot of fleas have bitten me.

I suppose hordes of fleas like these

live in the platform.

Look at that! The man wearing an air-raid hood

is scratching his arm as he sleeps.

Another man putting his helmet by his bedside

is scratching the scruff of his neck.

駅長は旅客のこの難渋を気づかないのか
僕もここの駅長を知つてゐる
松江の駅から今年栄転した
別所忠雄といふ人だ
去年　僕が松江に行つたとき
別所忠雄は駅の防空演習をずらかつて
僕を骨董屋に案内してくれた
ぼてぼて茶碗を買ふのだが
七軒も骨董屋を歴訪し
どの店でも薄茶を飲まされた
おかげで僕は吐きさうになつた
おい　もう一枚毛布がほしいな
子供の枕元にトランクを置いとくかね
さうだ　風よけの屏風だよ
寒いなあ　この風は海風なんだらう
おい　また蚤だ
僕は田舎の家に落着いたら
別所忠雄に手紙を出してやらう
「プラットホームを掃除しろ
清潔を保て」と書いてやらう

（鳥取駅から津山に出る車中しるす）

"Sweep the platform clean and keep it clean for keeps."

(Written in a train just leaving Tottori Station for Tsuyama Station)

# 水車は廻る

笹野顧六といふ牧師がゐる
笹野氏は篤心たる牧師です
僕の学生時代の知りあひです
そのころ師は神学校の生徒でしたが
学校を怠けて戯曲の習作に耽つてゐた
書きあげた原稿を古新聞に包み
僕のところに持つて来て読んでゐた

笹野君は「本読み」と称してそれを読んだ
今から四十年ちかく前のことである
僕はたいていその内容を忘れたが
たつた一つ覚えてゐる
「水車と加藤清正公」といふ脚本だ
──舞台右手に水車小屋がある
大きな水車が音もなく廻つてゐる
これは天地の悠久を暗示する──

# A WATER WHEEL GOES AROUND

There's a pastor named Koroku Sasano.
Mr. Sasano is a devout pastor.
He is an old acquaintance from my school days.
He was then a student at a divinity school
but was absorbed in writing plays, skipping school.
When it came to finishing one, he wrapped the MS in
an old newspaper, brought it to me and read it aloud.

Sasano-kun read it out loud, calling it "reading the script".
That was almost forty years ago.
I almost forget about the contents
but one thing is still clear in my mind.
It was a script entitled "A Water Wheel and Lord Kiyomasa
    Kato"
— there's a water wheel stage right.
The big water wheel is turning around without sound,

そこへ物具つけた加藤清正公が現はれる

紺色の垂衣に紺糸縅の鎧を着け

銀色に光る烏帽子型の兜をかぶり

黄金づくりの太刀を佩き

音に聞えた片鎌槍を携へてゐる


その出でたちは実に剛毅である

天晴れ大将軍の貫禄だが

舞台正面に出て来ると

「ああ脱糞したい」と独白する

次に「もういけねえ」と泣声を出し

瞑目して「ビチビチビチ……」と独白する

それで静かに幕である


笹野君は朗読後に傑作だと自讃した

表現派の戯曲だと云つた

僕は何のことだと思つたが

いまだにこの脚本だけは覚えてゐる

先夜も不図この筋書を思ひ出し

夢うつつに現在の師に思ひを馳せた

which signifies never-ending heaven and earth —

Lord Kiyomasa Kato clad in full armor appears.
He is wearing a dark blue garment under a suit of armor,
a shining-silver type of warrior's helmet,
and a short sword of gold work.
He is carrying a well-known cruciform spear, as well.

Attired as a warrior, he exudes an indomitable spirit.
Looking dignified like an admirable big shogun,
he says in a soliloquy, "Oh, I wanna defecate"
after he moves to the center of the stage.
Next his voice turns tearful. "Ooooh, it's all over."
He says again in a soliloquy with his eyes shut, "Brrr…brr…"
as the curtain is quietly lowering.

He praised himself as a masterpiece playwright after
    reading it and called it an expressionist play.
I had no idea what it was all about
but I still remember this script even now.

師よ　せいぜい神に祈り給へ

I happened to remember this plot the other night and dreamily turned my thoughts to his present status as a pastor. My master, pray to God as much as you can, anyway.

# 夜 の 横 町

文芸家協会の懇親会の帰り
マーケット横町を歩いてゐると
前方から新庄嘉章がやつて来た
「やあムツシユー　しばらく」
「やあ　今晩は」
いきなり新庄君は外套をぬぎ
両手にかざして左右に飛びまはるのだ
何の真似か
まさしくこれは闘牛士の真似だ
赤い毛布で猛牛をじらす真似である
右に飛び左に飛び
その目まぐるしいフツトワークは
さながら五条の橋の牛若丸だ
──だが何の意味か
こちらを牛にたとへての仕業である
悲しいかな聯想の行方

# A BYSTREET AT NIGHT

On my way back from a get-together of The Japan
Writers' Association I was walking down Market Bystreet
and saw Yoshiakira Shinjo ahead walking my way.
"Oh, Monsieur! Long time no see."
"Yeah, good evening!"
Shinjo-kun abruptly took off his mantle
and skipped from side to side holding it up with both
  hands.
What does he think he's doing?
No doubt he was playing the toreador.
It was the act of irritating a fierce bull with a red rug.
Hopping to the right, hopping to the left,
it's the dizzying footwork of a Ushiwakamaru standing
on the parapet of Gojo Bridge like a tightrope walker.
— But what's the meaning behind all this?
It's his way of comparing me to a bull.

こちらは牛のやうに太つてゐる
「ずゐぶん太つたね」と云ふ代りに
当意即妙　闘牛士の真似……
不思議に人通りのすくない夜であつた

（ハーモニカ横町にて）

The direction of this associated idea is pitiful.

No doubt I am fat as a bull.

Instead of saying, "You've grown fat as hell,"

he improvised his witty bullfighter bit right on the spot…

Strangely, it was the night when there were few people

on the street.

(At Harmonica Bystreet)

## 陸稲を送る

ふるさとの木下夕爾君の詩「ひばりのす」を
読んで、東京荻窪の陸稲の穂をふるさとの近
江卓爾君に送る。


この手紙に陸稲(をかぼ)の穂を同封します
たつた一と穂だが君に送ります
去年の秋の陸稲です


僕のうちから荻窪駅へ出る途中
東京衛生病院といふ病院がある
そこの前が広い空地になつてゐる
毎年その一部が陸稲畠に仕立てられ
秋になると「雀のおどし」が掛けられる
案山子(かかし)の立つ年もある


去年の秋はその陸稲が豊作でした
よく実つて重たげに穂を垂れてゐた

# SENDING RICE GROWN IN A DRY FIELD

After reading the poem "A Skylark's Nest"
by Yuji Kinoshita, a poet in my hometown,
I'll send an ear of rice grown in a dry field in
Ogikubo, Tokyo, to Takuji Omi in my hometown.

Enclosed in this letter please find rice grown in a dry field.

I'm sending you just one ear of rice,

which was harvested last autumn.

There's a hospital called Tokyo Adventist Hospital

between my home and Ogikubo Station.

A large vacant lot spreads out in front of that hospital.

A part of it is cultivated as a rice field every year

and 'a bird rattle' is hung in autumn

or a scarecrow takes its place in one year or another.

Last autumn there was a bumper rice crop there.

It ripened well, hanging its ears down heavily.

僕はその畠のほとりを通るとき
あまり見事な出来なので
君に送らうと穂を一つもらつて来た
ここに同封の穂がそれなのだ

僕の郷村には陸稲がない
なぜ畠に稲を植ゑないんだらう
僕は年来それが腑に落ちなかつた
もし君に陸稲をつくる気があれば
この穂を種子にしませんか

僕はこれを手文庫に入れたまま
今まで君に送るのを忘れてゐた
けふ木下君のよこした詩を読んで
ついうつかりしてゐたと気がついた
木下君の詩は「ひばりのす」と題されて
左記のごとく可愛らしい

When I passed by that cultivated land

I was given an ear of rice when telling the farmer how
fine it was.

That was meant for you and enclosed here it is.


There's no dry field rice in my hometown village.

I don't know why they haven't planted field rice.

I've been wondering about that for a long time.

If you happen to feel inclined to farm rice,

will you try using this ear of rice as a seed?


As a matter of fact I put it in a small box primarily for

storing letters and forgot to send it off to you.

I happen to read Kinoshita-kun's poem today

and was reminded that I forgot to send it to you.

Kinoshita-kun's poem "A Skylark's Nest"

is charming:

## ひばりのす

ひばりのす
みつけた
まだ誰も知らない

あそこだ
水車小屋のわき
しんりようしよの赤い屋根のみえる
あの麦ばたけだ

小さいたまごが
五つならんでる
まだ誰にもいわない

僕はこの詩で君のことを思ひ出した
陸稲のことにも気がついた

君のうちの庭は広かつた
それが空地利用で麦畠になつた

## A Skylark's Nest

No one knows yet
that I've found
 a skylark's nest.

Over there
by the water mill
in that wheat field
it's visible beyond the red roof of a clinic.

I won't tell anyone
that it contains
five small eggs.

This poem reminded me of you
and that is why I noticed that dry-field rice.

The garden in your house was spacious.
It became useful as a wheat field.

あのとき君の唯一の楽しみは
いまに雲雀が巣をかけて
卵が宿るといふことだつた
あの畠に陸稲はどうだらう

この稲は農林何号といふ名前か
つい迂闊なことに聞きもらした
今は調べる手数を省くとして
仮に荻窪一号とでも呼びたまへ
では今年の秋の豊穣を祈ります

Your only pleasure at that time
was that a skylark built a nest
and laid eggs there.
What about a rice crop instead of that wheat field?


I wonder if this rice was named 'agriproduct number-
    something.'
I wasn't paying attention and didn't catch the name.
Oh, I'll just save the trouble of checking
and call it 'Ogikubo number one', tentatively.
I'll pray for a prolific rice crop this autumn.

# 紙凧

私の心の大空に舞ひあがる
はるかなる紙凧　一つ
舞ひあがれ舞ひあがれ
私の心の大空たかく舞ひあがれ

# PAPER KITE

A single paper kite far in the distance
soars up into the wide blue sky of my heart.
Fly up, fly up in the air
and fly up high in the wide blue sky of my heart.

# あ　の　山

あれは誰の山だ
どつしりとした
あの山は

# THAT MOUNTAIN

Whose mountain is that?
That bulky and heavy
mountain?

# 泉

　　　　岡の麓に泉がある。



その泉の深さは極まるが
湧き出る水は極まり知れぬ

# SPRING

There's a spring at the foot of a hill.

The depth of the spring is shallow.
But it gushes water endlessly.

# 石　　垣

僕の記憶の間違ひだらうか
どうも不思議である


関東大震災の直後のことだ
僕は焼野原の街趾を通りぬけ
竹橋附近をとぼとぼ歩いてゐた
ふと濠の向うの大石垣に目をとめた


いつ見ても堂々たる石垣である
特にその日は大きな大きな大石垣に見えた
石組は型通り荒切石の布積みで
天場の縄だるみが石垣全面に気品を与へ
三ツ角の鳶口と宮勾配が鋭く取組んでゐる
かつて名城の誉れを助長した石垣だが
合点の行かぬことが一つあつた
縄だるみの中央直下に当つて少し右寄りに

# STONE WALL

Is it a confusion of my memories?
There's something strange.

It was about the time just after the Great Kanto Earthquake.
I was walking through a burned-out area where a town
had been and was plodding wearily down around
Takebashi when I suddenly noticed that big stone wall
    beyond a moat.

It was as imposing a presence as ever.
But on that day it looked bigger and bigger than before.
The rockwork was a typical range masonry of rough-
    cut rocks.
A sacred straw festoon on the top lent an air of dignity
    to the whole.
This stone wall was the outcome of cooperation

はつきり四ツ目積みにしてゐる箇所がある
なぜこんな不良な積みかたをしたものか


江戸城の石垣は徳川家康威令のもとに
西国大名が各個基準によつて普請を受持つた
歴史の本にそんな風に書いてある
すると竹橋辺から見て正面の石垣は
どこの何といふ大名が受持つたか


その大名は大御所の御機嫌を損じなかつたらうか
普請奉行は屹度お叱りを受けなかつたらうか
僕はさう思つた
しかし物には裏と表がある
和漢の倫理によれば憚る精神が大事であつた
金甌無欠を念ずるは畏れ多いことであつた
だから一箇所だけ手を抜いておいたのだらうか


その後この石垣のことは忘れてゐた
大震災以来だから五十年を経過した
その間その辺を通るときも念入りに石垣を見た

between a fireman's ax and temple carpentry.

And in the end it helped to win fame as an excellent castle but one thing puzzled me a lot.

Just a bit right of center of the straw festoon, down below there was a fourth rock standing out in the stone wall.

I wondered why a builder had done such clumsy work.


The stone wall of Edo Castle was built by daimyos in western provinces who were given an authoritative order by Ieyasu Tokugawa, the shogun.

A history book tells us all this.

As for the front stone wall seen just from around Takebashi, which daimyo or who was responsible for it?


Didn't that daimyo irritate the shogun?

Didn't the province commissioner in charge of castle construction receive a heavy punishment?

That's how I felt about it.

But there are two sides to everything.

According to Japanese and Chinese ethics

ことはない
ところが先々月の末に神田の古本屋を訪ねた
その帰りに竹橋附近で久しぶりに石垣を見て
何とも不思議に思つた
四ツ目積みのところは一つも見つからない
つくづく見ても見つからない
石垣を修理したあとも見つからなかつた

the prudential spirit is precious.

Wishing for a golden jug without a glaze was asking
    too much.

Was that the reason why they did poor work on only
    one detail?


I had forgotten about this stone wall after that.

Ever since the Great Kanto Earthquake fifty years have
    passed.

During that period I haven't looked at it carefully as I
    passed by.

But later I visited an old bookstore in Kanda and on my

way home I saw the stone wall from around Takebashi
    again and thought how strange it was.

I didn't find the fourth rock to be any different from
    the others; didn't find it as it had been before

however closely I looked.

I didn't find any sign of the mending of the wall, either.

# 誤　　　診

医者が僕のレントゲン写真を出して
「心臓肥大です、要注意ですな」と云つた

僕は尋常一年のとき運動会で駈けつこに出た
すると「用意、どん……」の直前
不意に胸がごつとんごつとん鳴りだした
これが僕の記憶する最初の胸の高鳴りだ

最近は胸のときめきを感じることがなくなつた
原稿書いてゐて胸がふと動悸を搏ちだすことな
　　ど更らにない
僕の感動の最後助<ruby>最後助<rt>さいごのすけ</rt></ruby>だと思はれるのは
京竿で一尺<ruby>山女魚<rt>やまめ</rt></ruby>を釣つたときのものである

僕の心臓は干涸らびてしまつてゐる筈だ
心臓肥大とは誤診だと思ひたい

# MISDIAGNOSIS

A doctor showed me my X-ray and said,
"Hypertrophy of the heart. You need special attention."

I participated in a running race in an athletic meet
as a first grader and just before "Get set! Go!",
my heart suddenly began thumping against my ribs.
This was my first heart-stopping experience
    as far as my memories go.

I haven't felt any fluttering these days.
I haven't had my heart start palpitating in writing a
    manuscript, either.
As far as my strong emotions are concerned,
the last time was when I caught a foot-long cherry salmon
    with my antique fishing rod.

My heart must have dried up by now.

I hope hypertrophy of my heart was my doctor's
misdiagnosis.

# 蟻　地　獄

（ コンコンの唄 ）


小学校へあがる前のこと──
お寺の廻廊の下が涼しかつた
そこの地面に二つ三つ蟻地獄の穴があつた
その穴のわきに身を伏せて
その穴にそつと頬を近づけて囁くのだ
「こんこん出やれ、鬼出やれ
　こんこん出やれ、鬼出やれ」
さう囁きながら
穴のわきを静かに静かに手のひらで叩く
これは一人遊びの遊戯である

それを私はお寺の小僧から教はつた
「こんこん出やれ、鬼出やれ」
繰返し囁き繰返し叩いてゐると
穴の底から蟻地獄が顔を覗かすのだ

# ANT LIONS

### (A Song of Gushing Water)

It was around the time before I entered primary school —
it was cool down under the cloister of a temple.
There were a few ant lion holes in the ground there.
I used to lie down beside the holes
and, putting my head closer to them, whispered:
"Come out in a whoosh! Come out, Ogre!
Come out in a whoosh! Come out, Ogre!"
Whispering those words,
I tapped each hole quietly and softly with my palm.
This was a game played by myself.

I was taught that game by a young monk in the temple.
"Come out in a whoosh! Come out, Ogre!"
While I repeatedly whisper and tap,
an ant lion is supposed to come out to play

兜の鍬型のやうな頑丈な顎を出し
「おい、いたづらは止せ」と云ひたげにすぐ隠れる
それを見て子供一人で遊ぶ遊戯であつた

and extend the hoe-shaped helmet crest of its firm jaws.

It seemed to be saying, "Hey, don't play a trick on me"

and immediately hid.

That being the case, it was a game a child played by himself.

# 冬

三日不言詩口含荊棘

昔の人が云ふことに
詩を書けば風邪を引かぬ
南無帰命頂礼
詩を書けば風邪を引かぬ
僕はそれを妄信したい

洒落た詩でなくても結構だらう
書いては消し書いては消し
消したきりでもいいだらう
屑籠に棄ててもいいだらう
どうせ棄てるもおまじなひだ

僕は老来いくつ詩を書いたことか
風邪で寝た数の方が多い筈だ

# WINTER

*Say nothing about poetry for three days and you'll feel*
*like you have a thorn stuck inside your mouth.*


As an old man used to say,
you can't catch cold if you write poetry.
*Pray devoutly to Buddha by putting your head on His feet.*
You can't catch cold if you write poetry.
I want to believe it blindly.


It's all right, though it isn't necessary to be stylish.
I write something and erase it and over and over again.
It would be all right even if I erased it and let it be.
It would be all right even if I threw it into a wastebasket.
Anyway throwing it away is a magic formula for warding
off bad luck.

今年の寒さは格別だ
寒さが実力を持つてゐる
僕は風邪を引きたくない
おまじなひには詩を書くことだ

I wonder how many poems I've done so far, reaching this age.
The number of times of being sick in bed with a cold
   must be greater.

It's especially cold this year.
The cold is really penetrating this year.
I don't wanna catch cold.
I've got to write poetry like that magic formula says.

# あとがき
## AFTERWORD

ユーモアあふれる詩人とか詩集を二つ三つ挙げて
みなさいといわれて、即座に答えられる詩の読者は
ほとんどいないのではないだろうか。もしも笑いを
誘発し面白おかしくさせてくれるような詩だけをそ
れが指しているなら、ユーモアあふれる詩人や詩集
が世に出回っている数は常に品不足の状態である。
詩人のペンに訴えかけようとするものは、もちろん
それなりの理由があって、疫病、災禍、死が強い力
を持っているのはいうまでもない。たとえば英語圏
の詩人、エミリ・ディキンソンのすばやい辛辣な棘
のある言葉、オスカー・ワイルドのいくぶん上から
目線のユーモア、e. e. カミングズの実験的かつ頭脳
的なユーモアといったようなさまざまな形で、ユー
モアは生まれてくるが、幅広い基準や種類を持ち合
わせたユーモア詩人を見つけるのは至難の業である。
至難の業であるが、それでもごく少数のまれびとが
いる。

Few are the readers who could readily name, if asked, even two or three humorous poets or poems. If by definition you simply mean poems that cause laughter or amusement, then indeed humorous poets and poems have always been in short supply. As is obvious, disease, disaster and death primarily appeal, for good reason, to the pens of poets. Even though humor comes in various forms such as the amusing quick barbs of Emily Dickinson, the high social humor of Oscar Wilde, and the experimental heady humor of e. e. cummings, humorous poets of any level or kind are uncommon — uncommon but there are some.

ユーモアの視点から日本の詩人の名前を挙げると、そのなかに、やさしさと傍若無人ぶりと可能性と荒唐無稽ぶりが入り混じったユーモアの詩集『よしなしうた』（青土社、1991 年）の作者、谷川俊太郎も含まれる。この『よしなしうた』と井伏鱒二の『厄除け詩集』とは、まったく隔たった地平に立つものであるとは限らない。井伏の詩は、日常の事物と人物と出来事を題材としながら、それらを非日常へと変える言葉の力を持っている。「水たまりにこぼれ落ちたつくだ煮の小魚達」、「もうすっかり濡れている石地蔵」、「『歳末閑居』の屋根にのぼる拙者」は成り行きの展開で、別のジャンルで文脈の違いはあっても、いくぶんチャップリン描く映画のひとコマに似ている。これに異議を唱えるひとは、チャップリンの芸術は高度に構成が意識され極度に明確な輪郭をぼかしているので、井伏の詩法と詩には当てはまらないというだろう。

Any naming of Japanese poets with a humorous touch must include Shuntaro Tanikawa whose *Songs of Innocence* (Seidosha, 1991) contains humorous poems both gentle and impertinent, both terrible and preposterous. Those poems are not altogether different from the poems in Masuji Ibuse's *Poems of Exorcism*. Ibuse's poems take ordinary objects and ordinary people and ordinary events, and render them extraordinary. Whether fish fall in a puddle, a stone Jizo is 'soaked to the skin' or a man astride his roof is found to be not at home, these are turns of event which in another medium, another context, are even somewhat Chaplinesque. The demurrer would be that Chaplin's art is highly structured and conceals a fairly hard edge, and neither of these characteristics applies to Ibuse and his poems.

井伏のおそらく自ら厄払いをしようとする詩群に
ふさわしいキーワードは、なんといっても「親しみ
やすい」である。親しみやすいばかりか、「心奪わ
れる」磁力を持っている。この詩を書いた詩人に対
し全幅の信頼を寄せていい。愛すべき作者の人柄が
にじみ出ている。ひとつひとつ丁寧にていねいに読んで
いくと、断じて失望させられないことが即座に感じ
取れるはずである（例外はひょっとしたら、煙管の
やにを丸薬にひねり口に押しこまれたかわいそうな
「蛙」だろう！）。現実的なのに超自然で、ときどき
シュールレアルなものが不気味なものに接近しなが
ら、さりげないものにも魔力が潜んでいて、人間と
いうものの正体を暴き出すのである。さらに読後も
ずっと何カ月もの間、詩はそっと心の奥の隅っこの
部屋に棲みついて離れようとしないのである。井伏
の詩はおかしくてついくすっと笑ってしまうが、同
時に薄気味悪い感覚に捕らわれる。この途切れのない
詩の源泉の魅力こそ、井伏鱒二の独壇場なのである。

ウィリアム・I・エリオット

西原克政

Of several possible keywords applicable to Ibuse's perhaps self-exorcising poems, one is 'approachable.' Not only approachable but 'inviting.' You trust the man who wrote these poems. He is lovable and reading poem after poem you quickly find that you are never disappointed (with the possible exception of the poem in which a poor frog suffered to have a nicotine-coated medicinal pill stuffed in its mouth!). Real but fey, sometimes the surreal leading towards the uncanny, some power is lurking in the casual unveiling of what a human being is; furthermore, the poems quietly haunt the halls of the heart even months after re-readings. Ibuse's poems precipitate chuckling and, it may be, a touch of the eerie. Such is the ongoing power of Masuji Ibuse.

William I. Elliott

Katsumasa Nishihara

本書は講談社文芸文庫『厄除け詩集』
（1994 年発行）を底本といたしました。

**井伏鱒二**（1898-1993）

広島県深安郡加茂村（現、福山市加茂町）出身。小説家。
本名は井伏満寿二（いぶしますじ）。中学時代より画家を
志すが、大学入学時より文学に転向する。『山椒魚』『ジョ
ン万次郎漂流記』（直木賞受賞）『本日休診』『黒い雨』（野
間文芸賞）『荻窪風土記』などの小説・随筆で有名

**ウィリアム・I・エリオット**（1931- ）

アメリカ、カンザス州出身。詩人、批評家、翻訳家。谷
川俊太郎の詩集 64 冊の英訳という現在までの膨大なライ
フワークは岩波書店の電子書籍で読める。1968 年から関
東ポエトリ・センターを創設し海外と日本の詩人の交流
につとめてきた。最新詩集に『DOWSING』がある。

**西原克政**（1954- ）

岡山県出身。翻訳家。著書に『アメリカのライト・ヴァ
ース』。訳書に『THE SINGING HEART』『えいご・のはら
うた』『定本 岩魚』『谷川俊太郎の詩を味わう』などがある。
谷川俊太郎の詩集の英訳を現在まで 8 冊岩波書店の電子
書籍で刊行。R.H. ブライス『川柳』近刊予定。

田畑書店

対　訳
厄除け詩集

2023 年　7 月　5 日　第 1 刷印刷
2023 年　7 月 10 日　第 1 刷発行

著　者　井伏鱒二
訳者　ウィリアム・I・エリオット／西原克政

発行人　大槻慎二
発行所　株式会社 田畑書店
〒 102-0074　東京都千代田区九段南 3-2-2　森ビル 5 階
tel 03-6272-5718　fax 03-3261-2263

装幀・本文組版　田畑書店デザイン室
印刷・製本　中央精版印刷株式会社

《ポケットスタンダード・シリーズ》

# これは水です

思いやりのある生きかたについて
大切な機会に少し考えてみたこと

**デヴィッド・フォスター・ウォレス 著**

阿部重夫 訳

天逝した天才作家が若者た
ちへ遺した名スピーチ。ス
ティーブ・ジョブズを凌ぎ全
米一位に選ばれた珠玉の
メッセージ。
文庫判上製・1320 円（税込）